TALES ABOUT TAILS

Written By: Jacqueline Mack
Illustrated By: Jan Holloway

ISBN 0-88625-089-7

© 1985 Hayes Publishing Ltd.
Burlington, Ontario

Hayes Publishing Ltd., 3312 Mainway, Burlington, Ontario L7M 1A7

Have you ever considered
The tail of a whale
Who loves to swim in the sea?
Or thought how a monkey
Uses his tail
To travel from tree to tree?

Well, let's read some tales
About tails of whales
And peacocks and lions and friends.
On each page is a tale
Of an animal's tail
– And you have to guess how
it ends . . .

This tail belongs to a little guy
Who spends his time away up high;
Through the air he loves to sail,
Grabs bananas with his tail,
Loves to swing from tree to tree,
(He does it all so easily).
– Who is he?

You're right.
– a monkey!
It's lots of fun,
As you can see,
To be a monkey
In a tree.

This tail belongs to
a huge someone
Who's too big
to have much fun
(You see he weighs about a ton).
He's huge and wrinkly,
his skin is gray,
And when he walks
his tail will sway
While all around
the earth will shake
(Maybe you'll think
it's a great earthquake).
But there's no need
to be afraid –

. . . It's just an elephant parade.

This tail belongs to
a grumpy old chap
Who always seems to
be taking a nap.
He lies in the water,
or out in the sun,
But you'd better not think he
will be much fun.
If you see him smile,
You'd be wise to run

Because, you see, he's a crocodile.

Around the branch this creature bends,
It's hard to know where he starts or ends.
(He curls around like a garden hose –
At one end his tail, at the other his nose.)
He's often quite harmless,
But make no mistake,

You'd better stay clear
if you frighten a snake!

You'd be very sore
if you ever tried
To sit on this tail
and go for a ride.
You'd go up and down,
in great leaps and bounds,
Hopping high in the air,
then thumping the ground,
Up hills and through fields,
through bushes and weeds;
In forests and outback,
at very great speeds,
And then when you stopped
You'd get off and say "Oooh . . ."

I'm glad that I'm not a kangaroo!"

This tail belongs to a clever thief
who often causes farmers grief –
For they're afraid he's out to steal
Their chickens for his evening meal;
He sneaks away among the rocks,

Where you won't catch this cunning fox.

If I weren't me. I'd like to be
This gentle giant of the sea.
I'd swim down into the ocean deep
Then surface for my midday sleep.
If I saw you, I'd wave my tail,
Which means

That I'm a friendly whale.

This tail doesn't look very useful at all.
It curls in knots, and it's really quite small;
It's meant to be pink, but quite often it's brown,
Because it's been rolled in the mud on the ground.
The animal to which it belongs doesn't mind . . .

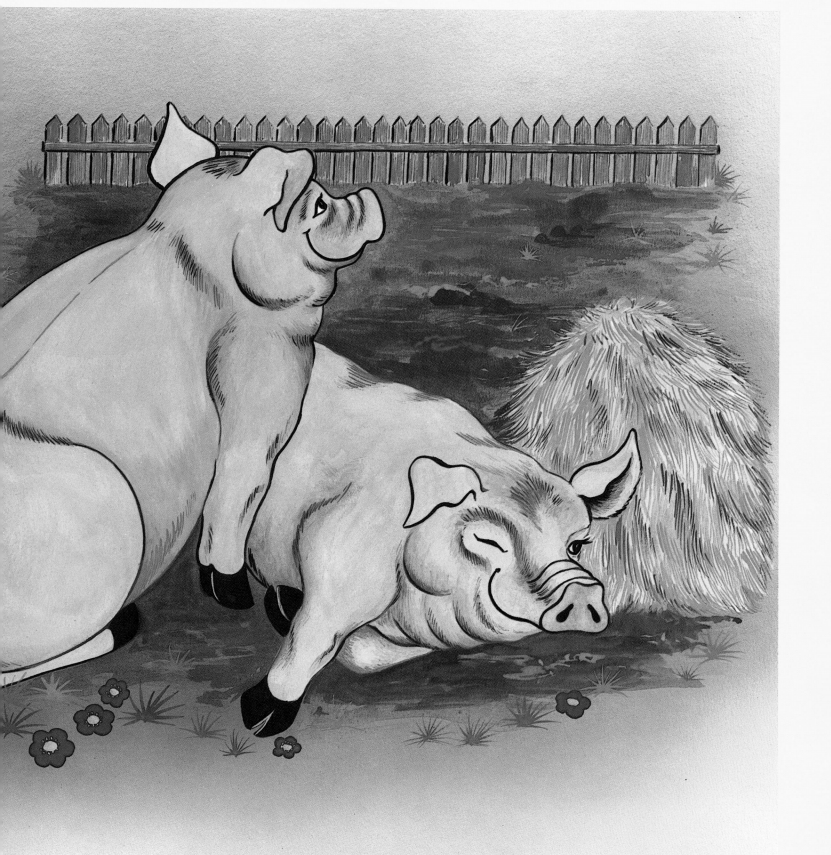

Because, to a pig, It's just its behind.

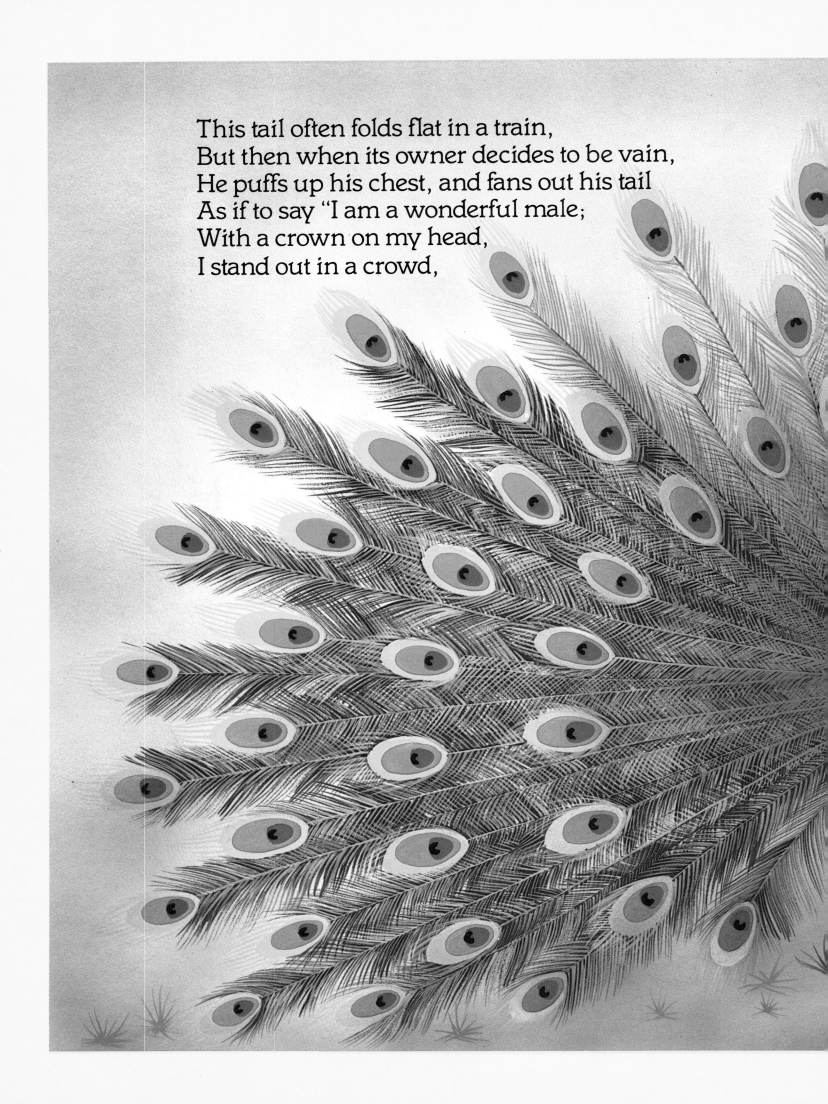

This tail often folds flat in a train,
But then when its owner decides to be vain,
He puffs up his chest, and fans out his tail
As if to say "I am a wonderful male;
With a crown on my head,
I stand out in a crowd,

I'm a beautiful peacock
– That's why I'm so proud."

By reading this book,
you've seen lots of tails
Of pigs and of monkeys,
of peacocks and whales;
But the tail on this last page
is far from the least,

Because it belongs
to the King of the Beasts;
He's fierce and he's brave,
and he's known to be proud,
And then when he roars,
he is really quite loud;
When he's sound asleep,
he's like a big cat,
But don't pull his tail,
and don't try to pat!
At the end of this tail
you'll find a great lion,
And this is the end of my
tale – no lyin'!

KE4 5 0
ABC De f